Have you read all these books in the Battersea Dogs & Cats Home series?

BAILEY'S story

CHESTER'S story

RUSTY'S story

MAX'S story

DAISY'S story

MISTY'S story

SNOWY'S story

❀ ❀ ❀ ❀

SNOWY'S
story

by

Sarah Hawkins

RED FOX

BATTERSEA DOGS AND CATS HOME: SNOWY'S STORY
A RED FOX BOOK 978 1 849 41303 9

First published in Great Britain by Red Fox,
an imprint of Random House Children's Publishers UK
A Random House Group Company

This edition published 2010

3 5 7 9 10 8 6 4

Set in 13/20 Stone Informal

Red Fox Books are published by Random House Children's Publishers UK,
61–63 Uxbridge Road, London W5 5SA

www.randomhousechildrens.co.uk

Addresses for companies within The Random House Group Limited
can be found at: www.randomhouse.co.uk/offices.htm

THE RANDOM HOUSE GROUP Limited Reg. No. 954009

A CIP catalogue record for this book is available from the British Library.

The Random House Group Limited supports The Forest Stewardship
Council® (FSC®), the leading international forest-certification organisation.
Our books carrying the FSC label are printed on FSC®-certified paper.
FSC is the only forest-certification scheme supported by the leading
environmental organisations, including Greenpeace. Our
paper procurement policy can be found at
www.randomhouse.co.uk/environment

Printed and bound in Great Britain by Clays Ltd, St Ives PLC

Turn to page 93 for lots
of information on the
Battersea Dogs & Cats Home,
plus some cool activities!

🐾 🐾 🐾 🐾

Meet the stars of the Battersea Dogs & Cats Home series to date . . .

Bailey

Misty

Chester

Rusty

Max

Daisy

Snowy

Christmas Shopping!

"Wow!" Lucy breathed as she looked up
at the biggest Christmas tree she'd ever
seen. It was in the middle of an
enormous department store; it was three
storeys high and covered with giant
baubles and fairy lights. Tinsel-wrapped
escalators led to more floors that sold
everything from fancy teapots to exercise
bikes.

"And Mum still can't find what she wants to buy!" Samuel, her twin brother, said, reading her mind as usual.

Christmas music was playing gently in the background, and the shop was packed full of people bustling past in thick winter coats, hats and scarves, looking for last-minute Christmas presents.

"What do you think of these?" Mum said as she hurried over, waving a pair of bright green socks with holly on them. Lucy screwed up her nose.

"Well we've got to find Great-uncle Tim *something*!" Mum said, then rushed off again.

Lucy jumped as a man dressed as an elf offered her a mince pie. "That boy over there nearly cleaned me out!" he grumbled. Lucy looked over at her brother, who had a mince pie in each hand and, by the looks of it, more than one in his mouth. Lucy bit into the yummy pastry as she went over to join him.

"Look at this, Luce," Samuel said, spraying crumbs everywhere. He knelt in front of one of the toy shelves and pulled a racing car onto his lap. "It's got turbo speed and everything!" he said, looking up at her with his eyes shining.

Lucy grinned, thinking about the exact same car that was already wrapped up at the bottom of Mum's wardrobe. They'd bought it months ago!

"Well you'll just have to wait and see what you get for Christmas," she teased. "Mum was going to get you a Barbie doll, but she *might* have changed her mind . . ." Lucy squealed as Samuel chased after her.

"Don't run around, you two, it's far too busy in here," Mum called, rushing up with loads of bags. She pulled out her shopping list and sighed. "I've just got three more shops to go to . . ." Samuel groaned loudly and even Lucy sighed. She liked Christmas shopping, but they'd been doing it for *hours*!

"Come on," said Mum patiently, "we've just got a little bit more to do and then we can go home and put up our tree."

Samuel and Lucy held hands as Mum led them down three escalators and out of the enormous shop.

Outside, the bright snowflake-shaped decorations of the high street gave off a twinkly light, and the air was crisp and wintery. Mum turned down a side road filled with little old-fashioned shops.

"Oh!" Lucy cried out as she passed one of them. In the bay window there was a beautiful snow scene. It had a little train running round a track that surrounded a toy village with snow-topped roofs. On one of the roofs there was a tiny model of

Santa's sleigh! Lucy and Samuel watched the train go round with their faces pressed to the windowpane.

"Come on, guys – in here," Mum called, going into the perfume shop next door. Samuel moaned and walked towards her like a zombie, dragging his feet.

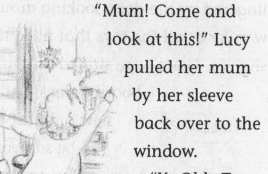

"Mum! Come and look at this!" Lucy pulled her mum by her sleeve back over to the window.

"Ye Olde Toy Shoppe," Mum said, reading the sign. "It's lovely! OK, well, why don't you both go in there while I'm next door finding a present for Aunt Ruthie? But look with your eyes, not with your hands!" she said,

raising her voice so Lucy and Samuel
could hear her over their cheers.

Lucy pushed open the toy-shop door,
which opened with a jingle. It was toasty
and warm inside, and it smelled like
mulled wine and Christmas spices.
Samuel raced into the shop, but Lucy
lingered by the door, looking around in
wonder at all the toys that filled the
shelves. There were stuffed animals, dolls,
board games – all brand
new and just waiting
to be someone's
Christmas present!

While she was staring, a funny noise caught her attention. Lucy turned round. To her right there was a big counter with a till on it, but there was no one there. There was another sound, a sort of snuffle this time, and Lucy bent down to peer underneath the counter. Hidden beneath it was a big tartan basket, and inside this was a brown and white dog with long floppy ears and big doleful eyes.

Lucy crept closer to it and put out her hand for it to sniff. "Hello!" she said. "Merry Christmas!"

"Merry Christmas!" came a voice back and Lucy gasped in surprise. There was a laugh from behind her and Lucy turned to face a kind-looking lady who was wearing a long skirt and a jumper with a reindeer on it. "Sorry, dear, I didn't mean to startle you," the lady continued. "That's Millie. She's had her Christmas presents early – look!" The lady opened the door of the counter to reveal the rest of Millie's basket. Huddled next to her were four *gorgeous* little puppies!

The Best Christmas Present Ever!

Lucy looked at the basset hound puppies in delight.

"They were born two weeks ago," the lady told her.

"They're *amazing*!" Lucy exclaimed, kneeling down to stroke them. "Sam, come and see this!"

"Cool!" Samuel breathed when he saw them.

"Do you want to hold one?" the lady asked. Lucy nodded furiously, and the lady scooped one of the little puppies out of the basket and put the squirming bundle on Lucy's lap. Lucy squealed happily as the little dog wriggled about and tried to suck her finger.

"If I had a puppy I'd call him Killer," Samuel said, cuddling one of the others.

Lucy looked at the tiny dog he was holding, which immediately gave a big puppy yawn.

"He's far too cute to have a name like that!" she told her brother. "I'd call him something nice, like Pickle."

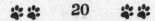

"Pickle!" Samuel made a face.

"I think Pickle's a lovely name!" came a voice from above. Mum had finished her shopping. "Honestly," she said, smiling at the lady, "I leave you two for a minute and you've made friends!" She put down her bags and bent to stroke the little puppy that was snuggled in Lucy's lap. "They are adorable though." She turned to the lady. "Are you planning on keeping them, or are they for sale?"

Lucy looked from her mum to her brother. Samuel's mouth had dropped open in amazement. Was their mum really asking if they could buy one of the puppies?

"I'm afraid we've already found homes for them all," the lady said.

Lucy looked at the little basset hound on her lap and sighed. For a minute there she had almost thought she'd be getting a puppy of her own. Samuel looked just as sad as they left the shop.

Mum walked a little way down the cobbled street and then turned to look at their gloomy faces. She pulled them both in for a hug. "Look," she said, "I need to talk to Dad, so no promises, but I think having a dog would be just lovely, and if you're willing to help out, well . . . well, I think we might be able to get one." Lucy and Samuel shrieked and hugged their mum tightly.

"You're crushing
the presents!" Mum
complained
laughingly.

"We don't
need other
presents!"
Samuel yelled.

"Because we're
getting a puppy!" Lucy finished.

"*Maybe*," Mum said warningly.

Samuel and Lucy talked about dogs all
the way home. Lucy even made them stop
off at the post office to see if there were any
puppies advertised on the notice board.
There was a bike for sale and a few adverts
for cleaners and babysitters – but no
puppies. Lucy was so excited about puppies
that she almost forgot that it was Christmas
in a few days. Samuel didn't though.

"You don't need to look at the board, Luce," he told her. "I've worked it out. Santa's going to bring us a puppy!"

If she hadn't been eating her advent calendar chocolates every morning, Lucy would have been sure that the next few days had actually lasted a week and a half. Finally, though, it was Christmas Eve. Lucy, Mum, Dad and Samuel played a game of Monopoly and watched a *Doctor Who Special* on TV that was so scary that Lucy had to hide behind the sofa and peek over the top.

"Right, bedtime, I think," Dad said as it finished.

Lucy groaned. "We haven't even put out a mince pie for Santa!"

"OK, but then up to bed," Dad said firmly.

Lucy and Samuel set out a mince pie and a carrot for Rudolph on a little tray, and Dad poured Santa a glass of whisky.

"Isn't Santa supposed to get sherry?" Mum asked him.

"No," Dad said seriously. "I happen to know that Santa likes a little drink of whisky as well. Anything to keep him warm while he's out on his sleigh," he added.

When the tray was all set out next to the fireplace, and Lucy and Samuel's stockings were hanging up neatly, Dad ushered them up the stairs and into their room. As Samuel climbed up to the top bunk of their bunk beds Lucy gave her mum a hug.

"It's Christmas tomorrow!" Mum said to Lucy, smoothing the duvet.

"Yay!" Lucy cried. "I'm too excited to go to sleep!"

"Ah, but the sooner you go to sleep, the sooner Santa will come." Dad grinned.

"Yeah, Luce, so shush," Samuel said, pulling the covers over his head.

"OK . . ." Lucy sighed. "But I'll probably be awake for ages . . ."

"As long as you're awake quietly, that's fine with me!" Mum laughed. "Goodnight, sweetheart. Goodnight, Sammy."

"Shhhh!" came a noise from Samuel's bunk.

Mum and Dad crept out of their bedroom, leaving the door open a crack so that the hall light came in. Lucy listened to them as they went back downstairs, and smiled as she heard her mum laughing.

"Sam?" Lucy whispered.

"Mmmm."

"Do you really think Santa will bring us a puppy?"

"He might do," her brother replied. "We'll find out tomorrow. If you ever go to sleep."

Lucy snuggled down under the duvet. She didn't think there was any way that she'd be able to sleep, but she shut her eyes anyway . . .

Christmas!

And suddenly it was morning. Christmas morning!

Lucy was woken up by Samuel clattering down the bunk-bed ladder. "Wake up, wake up, it's CHRISTMAS!" he yelled as he tore out of the room and down the stairs.

Lucy sprang out of bed and followed him. She ran into the lounge and gasped

at their stockings, which were bulging
with presents. Samuel had already taken
his down and was tearing into his first
gift.

"COOL!" he exclaimed, as he
unwrapped a toy dinosaur.

Lucy pulled her stocking down and
emptied it out onto the floor. There were
so many presents inside! Lucy was
squeezing the first one, which was
wrapped in pink spotty paper,
when her mum and dad
appeared in the
doorway.

"Merry Christmas!" Mum called sleepily.

"Mum, look what Santa brought me!" Samuel shrieked. Samuel was already surrounded by a mound of wrapping paper, the dinosaur, a Lego set, some socks and a new scarf.

Lucy tore into her first present. It was a beautiful bracelet. "Oh Mum, look at this!" she squealed, jumping up and showing her. Dad came in, handed Mum a cup of coffee and sat down to watch the twins' excited faces as they tore into their presents.

Soon Lucy had opened all her stocking

presents too, and the lounge was a big
mess of wrapping paper. Lucy looked at
her empty stocking and couldn't help
feeling a little bit sad. She had lots of
lovely things, but Santa hadn't brought
them a puppy after all.

She looked at Samuel,
and in the way that
sometimes
happened, Lucy
knew he was
thinking exactly
the same thing
as her.

Her brother put
his arm round her. "Let's give Mum and
Dad their presents," he whispered. She
gave a little nod, and Samuel grinned.

"Excuse me," he said, leaping up and
scattering toys and paper from his lap.

"Me too," Lucy added. "Back in a sec."

Lucy ran upstairs. Samuel already had their wardrobe open and was pulling the presents out of it.

"Mum's going to like mine better," he teased.

"No way!" Lucy told him. "I actually made mine, and you bought yours. Everyone knows home-made presents are better than shop-bought ones."

The twins raced downstairs and gave their parents their gifts. Mum loved the tea cosy Lucy had made her, although Dad joked that it was a hat and insisted

on wearing it on his
head, and she loved
the bubble bath
Samuel had bought.
Lucy gave Samuel the
racing car he'd wanted,
and he gave her a pair of
roller blades to replace the ones he'd
broken when he'd been pretending they
were tanks.

"You'll need to be careful with the
racing car," Mum told Samuel.

"Yes, Mum," Samuel replied, not really
listening.

"The puppy
might not like it,"
Mum continued,
winking at Lucy.

Lucy turned to her
mum, her eyes wide with surprise.

Samuel was distracted with his racing car. "I won't use turbo speed in the house," he said vaguely. Then he looked up. "Wait . . . what puppy?"

"The puppy Mum and I are getting you for Christmas," Dad chuckled.

"REALLY?" Samuel shouted.

"Really," Mum laughed. "We're getting a puppy!"

Lucy squealed, throwing a handful of wrapping paper up in the air and jumping around. Samuel joined her, and they did a little dance in the lounge.

"All right, all right." Mum smiled. "Be careful of your other presents."

"We don't need any other presents!" Lucy exclaimed.

"Lucy!" Samuel complained, clutching his racing car protectively.

"But where is the puppy? Is it wrapped up too?" Lucy said, looking around for a puppy-sized box.

"No!" Dad laughed. "A dog isn't just for Christmas, it's something we're going to have to love and look after for life.

We'll wait until Christmas is over and then we'll have time to think about what kind of dog we'd like and pick one from Battersea Dogs & Cats Home."

"That's a place where lots of dogs and cats are kept until they find nice homes," Mum told them. "Sometimes people give pets as Christmas presents without thinking about how the person they give them to can look after them, so Battersea Dogs & Cats Home has lots of pets brought to them after Christmas."

Lucy and Samuel didn't mind having to wait – they were just so excited that they were going to get a puppy of their very own!

Meeting Snowy

When Granny and Pops arrived for Christmas dinner, the twins rushed to tell them their exciting news!

"We're getting a puppy!" Lucy yelled as soon as they came in the front door, hugging Granny before she'd even taken her coat off.

All through Christmas dinner Samuel and Lucy talked about what the puppy

would be like. They
told their cousins
about the puppy on
Boxing Day, and they
told their other nana
on the phone.

They talked about
the puppy all over
the holidays, and
soon Lucy started
to get impatient.
She didn't want to
talk about the puppy
any more, she wanted him to be here! So
when Mum told them to get in
the car one morning, Lucy
had been a bit grumpy.

"I'm tired of visiting
people," she
complained.

"Who are we going to see today, boring Aunt Louise?" Samuel grumbled.

"Aunt Louise is *not* boring!" Mum replied sternly. "And if you two don't want to come, you can always stay at home and write your thank-you letters."

"No thanks," mumbled Samuel.

"Ready to go?" Dad called, climbing into the front seat. "Gosh, I would have thought that people on their way to find a puppy would look a bit happier than you do!"

So here they were in the car on the way to Battersea Dogs & Cats Home! Lucy was so happy she couldn't stop smiling. Samuel was so happy he couldn't stop talking!

"We're getting a Rottweiler called Beast," Samuel teased Lucy.

"No, we're getting a fluffy Pomeranian called Betsy," Lucy replied. "I want to dress *her* up."

"Beast."

"Betsy."

"*Enough*," Mum said firmly. "This dog is for all of us, and we'll decide together. Sam, the name Beast isn't suitable—"

"Ha!" Lucy laughed.

"And it's not very nice to dress a dog up, Lucy. It's a living creature, not a doll. How would you like it if we put you in funny clothes?"

"Right – we're here," Dad said, pulling into a road by Battersea Dogs & Cats Home. "And I want you both to be on your best behaviour."

"Beast," Samuel muttered as they got out of the car. Lucy stuck her tongue out

at him but she was too excited to argue. It was time to meet their puppy!

"Happy New Year!" The lady who met them at reception smiled, inviting them in.

"Now, I just have a few questions about your house and about you," she told them. "Just so we can make sure that we find your perfect pet. How much time do you have to exercise your dog?"

"I'll take him for a walk every day," Samuel told her.

"So will I!" Lucy interrupted.

"Gosh, I'm going to have to find you a dog that likes having lots of walks!" the lady said. "It's nice to see you know that having a dog takes a lot of time and energy. And love, of course."

"We know," said Samuel, and Lucy nodded furiously.

"And we know that a dog isn't just for Christmas," Lucy continued seriously. "But we've wanted a puppy for as long as we've been alive!"

"That's good to hear," said the lady, smiling.

"We won't return it or swop it for anything," Samuel added. "Not even a bike."

The lady led them over to the kennels. "I think I know just the dog for two such caring owners," she said, pointing into one of the cages. "This is Snowy."

Inside
the pen a
little puppy
was sitting
alertly. He
had brown,
white and
black patches
on his fur, and
his tail was all
brown with a
white tip. It was
wagging from side to side as if he was
already excited to see them! The lady
unlocked the door and they all went in.
Snowy bounded over and Samuel and
Lucy knelt down to stroke his soft fur.

"He is SOOOO adorable!" Lucy
whispered as she touched the wriggling
pup.

"He is cute," Samuel agreed, "but he's so small.

"He might be small now," Dad told him, "but he's a Saint Bernard and they grow up to be big dogs. Not that he's going to be allowed to attack anyone," he added hastily. "In fact Saint Bernards

were used as rescue dogs to help
find people if they got stuck in the
snow."

"So that's why he's called
Snowy!" Lucy smiled.

"That's right!" the lady told her.
"We very rarely see this breed of dog
at the Home. Snowy was left outside
reception by someone on Boxing Day,
like an unwanted present."

Samuel and Lucy looked
at each other and
then turned to their
parents. "We want
him!" they both
said at the same
time.

Fun in the Snow!

Two weeks later Samuel and Lucy burst out of school as fast as they could. "Race you!" Samuel yelled. Lucy pulled her hat down tightly on her head and rushed to catch up with her brother. They were desperate to get home because today was the day that Snowy was coming to live with them! A man from Battersea Dogs & Cats Home had come round to check that their house was suitable for him, and all was well.

"I've been reading the book Dad gave us about Saint Bernards," Lucy panted as she jogged beside Samuel. "It says that they need loads of exercise. He's going to need to be walked at least three times a day!"

"I'm not going to just take him for a walk," Samuel scoffed. "I'm going to take him exploring! That'll wear him out!"

"Oh, me too!" Lucy cried.

"Well, maybe." Samuel slowed down as they reached the garden gate. "But Snowy is a boy dog, you know. He's going to want to have boy adventures with me."

"Girls can have adventures too," Lucy said indignantly, shoving Samuel as they both tried to get though the gate at the same time.

"Get off!" Samuel moaned.

"MUM!" Lucy complained as the front door opened. But it wasn't Mum who came bounding out – it was a blur of brown and white – Snowy!

Snowy threw himself at Lucy and Samuel and began licking them all over, barking with joy.

"When he gets a bit bigger he'll knock you over if he does that!" came Mum's voice from the doorway. "I think someone needs some exercise. Put your school bags away and you can take him straight out for a walk."

"Yay!" Samuel and Lucy cheered as they stroked the excited puppy.

They dumped their school bags in a pile and clipped Snowy's lead on. It took both of them because he was squirming so much!

The twins walked Snowy round the corner to the local park. He was so excited at all the new sights and smells that he pulled hard on his lead. Lucy held onto it tightly and wondered how she'd manage when he was a *fully grown* Saint Bernard!

When they got to the iron gates that
led into the park they let Snowy off his
lead and he went dashing about
everywhere. First he
chased Samuel,

then
Samuel
chased him, and
then both of them chased
Lucy! Lucy had just flopped
onto the grass, laughing,
when she felt something
cold and wet land
on her nose.

She
looked up
and saw
snowflakes falling gently
from the sky.

"Look, Snowy – it's snow!" she cried. Snowy barked at the snowflakes as they fluttered down, faster and faster. Then he jumped up and snapped at them, trying to catch them in his mouth. One landed on his ear and he shook his head in surprise as it made his fur damp. Then he rolled over on the ground, digging his nose into the grass and pushing the fluffy white powder up into the air. Lucy scooped up some snow into a ball and threw it for Snowy to chase. Samuel made a snowball too – but he threw it at Lucy!

"Hey!" Lucy yelled, and grabbed some snow.

"Can't catch me!" Samuel yelled as she chased after him.

"Lucy! Sam!" came a voice from the path. It was Dad, holding two pairs of gloves. "Hello, Snowy!" he said as the puppy rushed over to him, barking.

"He's certainly living up to his name," Dad laughed. It was true – the little puppy was covered in snow! "Mum sent me to find you and bring you these," Dad said, handing them the gloves. Lucy took them gratefully – her hands were a bit cold from playing with the snow. "Mum's making hot chocolate," Dad told them, smiling. "Last one home has to find the marshmallows!"

Poor Lucy

It kept snowing all night, and the next morning when Lucy opened the curtains the back garden was a blanket of white.

"Snowy is going to love it!" Lucy told a sleepy Samuel, and ran downstairs to let the puppy outside. At first Snowy stepped in the snow uncertainly, lifting each paw up high before putting it down into the wet snow. But when Lucy and Samuel rushed out in their school uniforms and started throwing snowballs, Snowy soon joined in the fun.

"Let's make a snow *puppy*!" Samuel suggested. They made a pile of snow and Snowy ran round them excitedly. They were just shaping it into a body when, out of nowhere, Snowy ran forward and jumped right in the middle of the pile, scattering snow everywhere!

"Oh, Snowy!" Lucy laughed.

"Well, I suppose we don't need a snow puppy anyway," Samuel said, falling down next to Snowy and tickling the excited pup. "Not now we've got a real one!"

"Lucy, Sam! Come inside, you'll get cold!" Dad yelled from the kitchen window.

"It's time to go to school," Mum added as the twins wandered inside, grumbling loudly.

Lucy had drama club on Wednesdays, so it was half past four before she could leave school. She rushed out into the playground and stopped forlornly when

she
saw Mum
there without
a little brown
and white puppy
at her feet.

"Where's Snowy?"
she whined, feeling very upset.

"Sam's taken him for a walk,"
Mum replied. "They'll probably be
back by the time we get home,"
she continued, looking at
Lucy's sulky face.

"It's not fair!"
Lucy told her
unhappily.
"Snowy is
MY dog
too!"

"Snowy belongs to both of you," Mum said firmly, "and you're going to have to learn how to share him. There's plenty of him to go around," she joked, "and there'll be even more when he gets older and bigger!"

Lucy was still annoyed, especially when they arrived home and Samuel and Snowy still weren't back! She went straight upstairs and slumped on her bed.

Ten minutes later, Lucy heard Samuel come running through the front door, excitedly shouting about what a great adventure he and Snowy had just had. Lucy crept out of the room and went to the top of the stairs to listen.

"Snowy was brilliant! He picked up a scent and we followed it through a hole in the hedge and down to a secret stream. And by the stream was this broken boat, covered in plants. It looked really old," Samuel told his mum.

"It was probably a pirate ship! I'm going to go back there tomorrow and get some of the weeds off it – there might be a treasure map still in it! We're going to be rich and it's all thanks to Snowy!"

Hearing what a good time they'd had just made Lucy feel worse. She stomped back into her room and threw her pillow at the door, narrowly missing Snowy, who had come in to find her.

"Oh, sorry, Snowy," Lucy sobbed as she scooped him up onto her bed and cried into his soft fur. "Sam's always trying to leave me out," she sniffed. "But I won't let him. You're my dog too, and I love you just as much as he does."

Snowy snuggled into her arms and licked a salty tear from her face.

She heard Mum's voice from downstairs. "I'm glad you had a good time, but you've only just made it back before it got dark – and look, it's snowing again. Snowy is just a puppy – you have to be responsible for him. Plus, next time, it'd be nice if you took your sister with you . . . "

"Humpf," Lucy snorted. "I don't want to go along with him anyway. We can have our own adventures, can't we, Snowy?"

"Woof!" Snowy replied.

Just then
Samuel poked
his head round
the door. Lucy
turned over in bed so
that he couldn't see her
face. "Are you still sulking in
here, Luce?" Samuel said,
pulling a face at her. "I'll show
you the pirate ship tomorrow – don't
be a baby."

"I don't want to see your stupid pirate
ship," Lucy shouted.
"Snowy and I can
have much better
adventures on
our own! And
I'm exactly the
same age as
you!"

Lucy stayed upstairs all evening long. She could hear the others laughing downstairs, and Mum called to ask if she wanted to watch a DVD, but she didn't leave her room. Loyal Snowy stayed curled up next to her.

When Samuel came up to go to bed Lucy pretended to be asleep. She didn't even move when he took Snowy down to his basket, although from the way Snowy licked her face to say goodbye she felt sure the clever little puppy knew she was awake.

Lucy lay in bed thinking as Mum and Dad went to sleep and the house grew quiet. If only there was some way she could explore the pirate ship before Samuel did. That would show him. Then she had an idea. She could be first on the ship . . . if she went to find it *now*!

A Night-time Adventure

Lucy crept downstairs into the kitchen.
Snowy was curled up in his basket, but he
looked up when she came in and gave a
low whine. "We're going exploring,
Snowy!" Lucy whispered excitedly. "Right
now!"

Lucy went to the downstairs cupboard
and got her wellies and her coat, which
she pulled on over her pyjamas. Then she

spotted Dad's big torch on a shelf. "That might come in handy!" she whispered to Snowy as she fixed his lead onto his collar.

Lucy opened the front door – and stared in amazement. Snow was falling heavily, and it was cold and very, very dark. Maybe this wasn't such a good idea after all.

Lucy thought of Samuel, tucked in bed upstairs – he'd be so jealous when he found out that she and Snowy had been on a night-time adventure! Determinedly, Lucy and Snowy stepped out into the night.

The snow was already up to Lucy's ankles, and it took her and Snowy a long time to get to the park. Finally they reached the iron gates and Lucy bent down to give Snowy a cuddle. "Take me to the pirate ship, Snowy!" she told him.

She didn't unclip his lead – if he ran
too far away from her she might never
find him again in the dark – but
she let it out so that Snowy
could run ahead.

He raced
off and Lucy
followed, her heart beating
quickly. This was it, she was going to
get there first! Snowy was taking her to . . .
a tree. Snowy stopped at the tree and
sniffed all round it before lifting his leg
and doing a little wee in the fresh snow.

"No, Snowy!" Lucy sighed. "Find *the pirate ship*, by the stream. Do you remember the stream?"

Snowy cocked his head on one side and looked at her seriously as if he was listening. Then he jumped up and bounded into a pile of snow. Lucy groaned. They'd come all this way for nothing.

Lucy was just winding Snowy's lead up for the walk home, when Snowy suddenly started sniffing the air. Then he rushed towards a hedge at the far side of the park.

"What's up? Have you found the scent, Snowy?" Lucy asked excitedly.

"Woof!" Snowy barked proudly as he took her up to a hole in the hedge, and then disappeared through it.

"Good boy, Snowy! Wait for me!" Lucy
called as she scrambled through after
him. Snowy was down at the bottom of a
steep bank, barking happily as he
splashed about in the stream!
They'd found it!

Lucy slid down the bank
and paddled into the
water next to Snowy.

Apart from the friendly yellow circle of
torch light, everything was pitch black.
Trees waved their branches overhead, and
a noise in the bushes next to her made
Lucy feel suddenly nervous.

"Let's just find the boat and go home,"
Lucy told Snowy, sounding braver than
she felt. Snowy had stopped leaping
about and was carefully walking through
the stream next to her. Lucy was very
glad of the little dog's company.

Just as she was thinking that they
ought to turn back, Lucy noticed a
shape at the edge of the stream.
It was the ship.

It loomed out of the
water scarily, and Lucy
shuddered. It would be much
more fun to play on the ship in the
daylight with Samuel.

Lucy shivered, and realized how cold
she was. The snow was still falling and
water from the stream had got into her
boots and made her feet freezing.

"Come on, Snowy, let's go home," Lucy said. She turned to leave, but her leg caught on Snowy's lead and she stumbled – dropping the torch in the stream. The light went out – and suddenly it was completely dark.

Snowy to the Rescue!

"Oh no! Oh no!" Lucy muttered as she felt for the torch in the icy water. She couldn't see a thing! "Snowy, where are you?" she called.

"Woof!" Snowy replied. He bounded over to her and she wrapped her arms around his fluffy body. Snowy was shivering a bit too, despite his thick fur.

"Oh Snowy, I'm so sorry, I should

never have taken you out!" Lucy cried.
"Now we're lost out here and we'll never
find our way home in the
dark!"

Snowy
wriggled out of
her hug and
started barking.
"Help!" Lucy
yelled, but they
were in the middle of
the woods and there was no one to hear.

Snowy barked again. "It's no good,
Snowy," Lucy whimpered. The snow was
coming down even faster than before,
and her coat was almost covered. "We
can't stay still," she told the little dog.
"We'll turn into snowmen. Maybe we
should try and get back to the park.
There might be street lamps up there."

She turned and started scrambling up
the bank, feeling her way in the
darkness, but Snowy pulled on
his lead in the other direction.
When Lucy didn't follow
him he turned back and
pushed his head
against the back of
her leg and gave
one big "Woof!"
as if to say,
*Come on, I
know the
way!*

Lucy hooked her hand into Snowy's collar so that he could lead her. She stumbled along behind the little puppy, tripping on tree roots and nearly falling over lots of times. It was so dark that she could barely see Snowy at all! Then Snowy gave a bark and moved faster than before. Up ahead she could see a little bit of light coming from the hole in the hedge.

It was the park! Snowy galloped up the slope and Lucy climbed after him. "Oh thank you, Snowy!" she said, giving the pup an enormous hug. Snowy licked her face excitedly.

From the glow of the lampposts Lucy managed to find the way home. By the time they got back to the front door, she and Snowy were both exhausted, muddy and frozen through.

"Now we have to be quiet," Lucy whispered to Snowy as she opened the door. She brought him inside, and was just trying to use her numb fingers to take her wellies off, when the landing light clicked on. There, at the top of the stairs, looking half asleep, were Mum and Dad.

"Lucy! What are you doing up?" Mum gasped, rubbing her eyes in amazement. "Have you been outside?" she said as she ran down the stairs. "Oh, you're freezing." She looked at Dad. "Can you go and run a bath? And fetch a towel for Snowy too!"

With a flurry of activity Lucy's mum and dad had them both warmed up in no time.

Soon Lucy was sitting at the kitchen table in a cosy dressing gown, with a cup of hot chocolate and Snowy on her lap. She sighed happily, relieved to be home, then looked at her parents' cross faces and realized that she was still in BIG trouble.

"I'm sorry," she told them. "I just wanted to see the pirate ship so badly."

"You must never, ever do anything like that again," Mum said angrily. "It's so dangerous – anything could have happened to you."

"Something *did* happen!" Lucy told them. "The torch went out when I dropped it in the stream and if it wasn't for Snowy I would never have found my way home again."

"And then where would we be? We'd have lost you for ever!" Mum scolded her. "Thank goodness for Snowy." Mum and Dad made a big fuss of the little dog,

until his tail was wagging so
fast it was a blur!

"What's happening?" came a
sleepy voice from the door. Samuel
padded into the kitchen and Mum made
him some hot chocolate too. Lucy told
him all about her night-time excursion,
and Samuel's eyes grew wider and wider.

"Cool!" he exclaimed, looking at Lucy
with admiration.

"Not cool!" Mum said firmly. "Your
sister is in SO MUCH trouble, and so will
you be if you ever do something that silly.
Now off to bed, both of you."

"So, can I come with you on the next adventure?" Samuel asked Lucy when they were both tucked up in their bunk beds.

Lucy looked at Snowy, who was curled up on the end of her bed. "Yes," she said. "From now on we'll share all our adventures – and Snowy – equally. After all, he loves us both the same!"

Read on for lots more . . .

🐾 🐾 🐾 🐾

Battersea Dogs & Cats Home

Battersea Dogs & Cats Home is a charity that aims never to turn away a dog or cat in need of our help. We reunite lost dogs and cats with their owners; when we can't do this, we care for them until new homes can be found for them; and we educate the public about responsible pet ownership. Every year the Home takes in around 12,000 dogs and cats. In addition to the site in south-west London, the Home also has two other centres based at Old Windsor, Berkshire, and Brands Hatch, Kent.

The original site in Holloway

History

The Temporary Home for Lost and Starving Dogs was originally opened in a stable yard in Holloway in 1860 by Mary Tealby after she found a starving puppy in the street. There was no one to look after him, so she took him home and nursed him back to health. She was so worried about the other dogs wandering the streets that she opened the Temporary Home for Lost and Starving Dogs. The Home was established to help to look after them all and find them new homes.

Sadly Mary Tealby died in 1865, aged sixty-four, and little more is known about her, but her good work was continued. In 1871 the Home moved to its present site in Battersea, and was renamed the Dogs' Home Battersea.

Some important dates for the Home:

1883 – Battersea start taking in cats.

1914 – 100 sledge dogs are housed at the Hackbridge site, in preparation for Ernest Shackleton's second Antarctic expedition.

1956 – Queen Elizabeth II becomes patron of the Home.

2004 – Red the Lurcher's night-time antics become world famous when he is caught on camera regularly escaping from his kennel and liberating his canine chums for midnight feasts.

2007 – The BBC broadcast *Animal Rescue Live* from the Home for three weeks from mid-July to early August.

Amy Watson

Amy Watson has been working at
Battersea Dogs & Cats Home for six years
and has been the Home's Education
Officer for two and a half years. Amy's
role means that she organizes all the
school visits to the Home for children
aged sixteen and under, and regularly
visits schools around Battersea's three

sites to teach children how to behave and stay safe around dogs and cats, and all about responsible dog and cat ownership. She also regularly features on the Battersea website – www.battersea.org.uk – giving tips and advice on how to train your dog or cat under the "Amy's Answers" section.

On most school visits Amy can take a dog with her, so she is normally accompanied by her beautiful ex-Battersea dog Hattie. Hattie has been living with Amy for just over a year and really enjoys meeting new children and helping Amy with her work.

The process for re-homing a dog or a cat

When a lost dog or cat arrives, Battersea's Lost Dogs & Cats Line works hard to try to find the animal's owners. If, after seven days, they have not been able to reunite them, the search for a new home can begin.

The Home works hard to find caring, permanent new homes for all the lost and unwanted dogs and cats.

Dogs and cats have their own characters and so staff at the Home will spend time getting to know every dog and cat. This helps decide the type of home the dog or cat needs.

There are five stages of the re-homing process at Battersea Dogs & Cats Home. Battersea's re-homing team wants to find you the perfect pet, sometimes this can take a while, so please be patient while we search for your new friend!

1 Application

2 Interview

3 Home visit

4 Searching for a pet

5 Leaving with your new pet

Have a look at our website:
http://www.battersea.org.uk/dogs/ rehoming/index.html for more details!

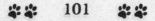

"Did you know?" questions about dogs and cats

- Puppies do not open their eyes until they are about two weeks old.

- According to *The Guinness Book of Records*, the smallest living dog is a long-haired Chihuahua called Danka Kordak from Slovakia, who is 13.8cm tall and 18.8cm long.

- Dalmatians, with all those cute black spots, are actually born white.

- The greyhound is the fastest dog on earth. They can reach speeds of up to 45 miles per hour.

- The first living creature sent into space was a female dog named Laika.

- Cats spend 15% of their day grooming themselves and a massive 70% of their day sleeping.

- Cats see six times better in the dark than we do.

- A cat's tail helps it to balance when it is on the move – especially when it is jumping.

- The cat, giraffe and camel are the only animals that walk by moving both their left feet, then both their right feet, when walking.

Dos and Don'ts of looking after dogs and cats

Dogs dos and don'ts

DO

- Be gentle and quiet around dogs at all times – treat them how you would like to be treated.
- Have respect for dogs.

DON'T

- Sneak up on a dog – you could scare them.
- Tease a dog – it's not fair.
- Stare at a dog – dogs can find this scary.
- Disturb a dog who is sleeping or eating.

- Assume a dog wants to play with you. Just like you, sometimes they may want to be left alone.
- Approach a dog who is without an owner as you won't know if the dog is friendly or not.

Cats dos and don'ts

DO
- Be gentle and quiet around cats at all times.
- Have respect for cats.
- Let a cat approach you in their own time.

DON'T
- Never stare at a cat as they can find this intimidating.

- Tease a cat – it's not fair.
- Disturb a sleeping or eating cat – they may not want attention or to play.
- Assume a cat will always want to play. Like you, sometimes they want to be left alone.

Here is a delicious recipe for you to follow.

Remember to ask an adult to help you.

Cheddar Cheese Dog Cookies

You will need:

227g grated Cheddar cheese

(use at room temperature)

114g margarine

1 egg

1 clove of garlic (crushed)

172g wholewheat flour

30g wheatgerm

1 teaspoon salt

30ml milk

Preheat the oven to 375°F/190°C/gas mark 5.

Cream the cheese and margarine together. When smooth, add the egg and garlic and mix well. Add the flour, wheatgerm and salt. Mix well until a dough forms. Add the milk and mix again.

Chill the mixture in the fridge for one hour.

Roll the dough onto a floured surface until it is about 4cm thick. Use cookie cutters to cut out shapes.

Bake on an ungreased baking tray for 15–18 minutes.

Cool to room temperature and store in an airtight container in the fridge.

Some fun pet-themed puzzles!

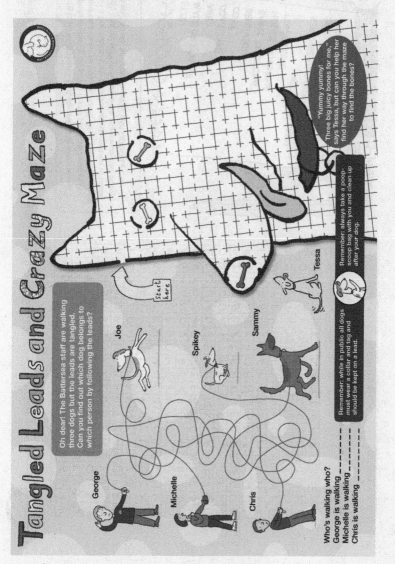

What to think about before getting a dog!

Here is a list of things that you need to think about before getting a dog. See if you can find them in the word search and while you look, think why they might be so important. Only look for words written in black. They can be written backwards, diagonally, forwards, up and down, so look carefully and GOOD LUCK!

SIZE
MALE OR FEMALE
AGE
COAT TYPE
COST
BEHAVIOUR
BASIC TRAINING
HOUSE TRAINING
TIME ALONE
GOOD WITH: PETS, CHILDREN,
STRANGERS, DOGS
HOW: ENERGETIC, CUDDLY,
STRONG WILLED, INDEPENDENT

Remember: when training a dog, reward works better than punishment.

Can you think of any other things? Write them in the spaces below.

Dog Breeds Crossword

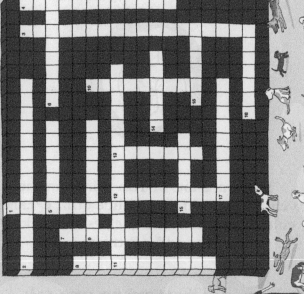

Across

2 A breed used as police dogs and sometimes called an Alsatian. (6,8)

5 A dog that is a mixture of breeds. (7)

6 A breed commonly used as guide dogs for the blind. (8)

9 Smallest breed of dog. (9)

11 A brown/liver and white breed often referred to as sniffer dogs. (8,7)

14 A French breed with very curly hair, traditionally used as a gun dog. (6)

15 A small black and tan terrier that was used to catch rats. (6)

16 A small white terrier from Scotland. (6)

17 A small breed with short legs and a long back, sometimes called a sausage dog. (9)

18 The dog often used as the symbol of Great Britain. (7)

Down

1 A spotted dog from a Disney film that needs lots of walking as a pet. (9)

3 A breed associated with a brand of paint. (3,7,8)

4 This breed is used to herd sheep and needs lots of activity such as agility if kept as a pet. (6,6)

7 Eddie from the programme Frasier is one of these. (11)

8 A breed associated with a brand of shoes. (6,5)

10 Scooby Doo was one of these very large dogs. (5,4)

12 These dogs are used for racing but also make good pets. (9)

13 Smaller version of 'Lassie' dog. (7)

Help!

Ali is trying to count the dogs but some of them keep running about.

How many can you count?

Remember: all dogs need exercise in order to keep them fit and healthy and to give mental stimulation.

111

There are lots of fun things on the
website, including an online quiz, e-cards,
colouring sheets and recipes for making
dog and cat treats.

www.battersea.org.uk